找烏龜
Money Turtle

中英雙語版

張江寧／著；姜硯庭／繪
Johnnie & John

欸你知道 **錢龜** 嗎？

就是那種，聽說只要擺一枚在錢包裡，財富之氣就會跟著你走的小東西。

但我們故事裡的錢龜，怎麼好像有點不一樣？

他好像有個名字、有點賴皮，還有一個偷偷的願望。

嗯該怎麼說呢？大概就是，嗯？他可以出現在這裡嗎？

Here in Taiwan, turtles are symbols of luck and longevity,

so sweets and charms are often shaped like turtles, like the Money Turtle, a coin-like charm.

People here believe that if you carry one in your wallet, money will follow you everywhere.

However, the money turtle in our story seems a bit different.

He seems to have a name and a purpose, and he's here on borrowed time.

Someone might say, "Wait a second, can he even be here?"

出門工作前一晚，她收到一盒花生糖，
底部附贈了個小錢龜。

The night before going to work, she received a box of peanut brittle.
At the bottom of the box was a money turtle – the kind old Asians carry
around for good luck with money.

小錢龜小小的，卻很亮，
老派可愛，所以她就收到錢包裡。
That turtle was small but shiny. Finding it cute,
she stuck it in her wallet.

瑪妮是個節目製作人。
許多年來，她說了許多明亮動人的故事
給小孩聽。

Marney is a children's TV producer.
For many years, she told sunny and touching
stories to kids around the world.

有一次，瑪妮受邀來到台灣演講，主辦方給她安排了隨行口譯。
不工作的時候，翻譯們就化身嚮導，帶著瑪妮東跑和西玩。

One time, she was invited to come to Taiwan to speak. The organizer provided her with translators. When they were not working, these translators would turn into guides, taking her on adventures around Taipei.

他們拜訪了富麗堂皇的故宮。

They visited the National Palace Museum.

他們品嚐了繁華熱鬧的夜市。

They ventured into the bustling night market to try delicious food.

他們走到了有落日、彩雲的平溪。

They walked to Pingxi to see the sunset and the beautiful clouds.

他們漫步在歲月靜好的老街。

They strolled through tranquil old streets.

還一起幫挪威的老阿公製作人過了生日呢！

Together they celebrated the birthday of an old Norwegian producer.

台灣有好多烏龜造型的糕點耶，
每次見了，瑪妮都搖搖頭微微笑，不收下。
翻譯們不知道瑪妮的故事，只以為瑪妮不喜歡甜。

There are many turtle-shaped pastries in Taiwan,
and every time someone offered Marney one, she would politely smile and decline.
People didn't know Marney's story; they simply assumed she didn't like sweets.

直到最後一天，在輕煙繚繞的月老廟前，
其中一名翻譯問瑪妮求不求紅線？

That's until the last day, in front of the temple of The Old Man Under the Moon,
one translator asked Marney if she would like to have a bundle of red thread –
the kind young Asians carry around for good luck in love.

瑪妮照樣搖頭微笑說不用，她順其自然就好。
但那天那個翻譯不放棄，她翻出錢包倒倒倒，倒出了一團紅線和小金龜。

As usual, Marney smiled and declined. But this time, her translator wouldn't give up;
she rummaged through her wallet and pulled out the red thread and a small
golden turtle, explaining that the red thread was small and no trouble.

剛好的陽光落在她手上，一切都有點閃閃發亮。
瑪妮停下了來，看著烏龜。

Sunlight fell on her hand,
and Marney's eyes rested on the shiny turtle.

「那是什麼？」
"What's that?"

「嗯？這是紅線啊。」
"Hmm? Oh, this is a red thread."

「不是，我是說旁邊那個。」
"No, I mean the thing next to it."

「喔這個啊，這是錢龜啦。」
"Oh, this? It's a money turtle."

翻譯抓抓頭，有點不好意思地說：
「這是上週朋友給我的，我剛好把他倆放在一起。」
The translator scratched her head and said, a little embarrassed, "A friend gave
it to me last week, and I happened to keep it with the red thread."

「等等等，所以，」
瑪妮問：「所以這一路上，小金龜都跟著嗎？」
"Has it always been with us during this trip?"

「嗯，還真的都跟著呢，」翻譯眼睛一亮，說：
「剛好就在你到台灣的前一晚收到。」
"As a matter of fact, yes.
I got it the day before you arrived."

「還早了一天嗎？」
瑪妮把小金龜拿在手裡，擦擦眼，笑了笑，
最後說：「我可以和你說個故事嗎？」
"One day early, isn't he?" Marney held the money turtle
in her hand, dabbed her eyes, and smiled.
She asked, "Can I tell you a story?"

瑪妮是個節目製作人。
但她卻一直有個大雨滂沱的故事，不怎麼對人說。
Marney is a children's TV producer.
For many years, she kept a rainy and grey story in her pocket and didn't tell it.

瑪妮的老公在五年多前去世了，在那之後，
她難過了好久好久，差一點點就找不到出口。
Her husband passed away five years ago,
and for a while, she was not okay at all.

直到有天，她發覺這樣不行，
於是瑪妮把自己踢出家門，到巴黎找朋友。
One day, she realized this cannot be.
So, she kicked herself out of the house and
went to Paris to visit a friend.

RIP
DUKE

但到了法國，上火車前，瑪妮卻害怕了。

Before she boarded her train to Paris, Marney hesitated.

等等等，等一下，如果她受不了怎麼辦？如果哭出來了怎麼辦？
瑪妮緊張兮兮，卻還是硬著頭皮走入車廂。

Wait, wait, what if this is too much? What if she couldn't take this after all?
Nervous, she still walked onto the train.

……卻馬上就愣住了。

因為火車廂的玻璃窗上，

有人塗鴉了大大的「杜克」兩字。

而「杜克」，正好就是瑪妮老公的名字呢。

看著塗鴉，瑪妮說不出話。

通往巴黎的火車有那麼多，

就偏偏、就剛好，

讓她走入了這一節車廂嗎？

...and froze right afterward.

For someone had scrawled "DUKE"
on the window glass.

And DUKE was exactly her late husband's name.

Wait, wait, wait, out of all the trains in Paris,

this is the one that she enters, after all?

像在遠在天邊、一望無際的沙漠裡看見希望。
Like spotting hope in a vast and endless desert, ever so slightly,

瑪妮輕到不行地在窗玻璃邊坐下，
摸摸玻璃、揉揉眼睛，找回了許久不見的安靜。
Marney sat by the window, feeling at last peaceful.

朋友來接瑪妮，說要帶她去一間新發現的好餐廳。
結果你猜猜餐廳的名字是什麼？

Marney's friend picked her up in Paris and suggested a new restaurant they had found.
Now, guess what the name of the restaurant is?

是「杜克餐廳」，圖騰還是革龜呢。

It's Duke's Restaurant with the logo of a leatherback turtle.

這下子瑪妮沒辦法了，她在大街上、眾人前，非常大聲地哭了出來。
因為杜克生前最、最、最喜歡的動物就是烏龜啊，
他從世界各地收集回了各式各樣的烏龜飾品。

Marney burst into tears in front of everybody
because the turtle was exactly her husband's favorite animal.
He had a collection of them from all over the world.

這巧合加上那巧合，簡直就像……就像杜克也知道，
也知道她正那麼努力，想走出來那樣。

With all these coincidences, it was as if... as if he was there with her.

從那以後，瑪妮就覺得，
只要見了烏龜，就是杜克在陪著她。
Since then, whenever Marney sees a turtle,
she thinks of Duke.

「……但很多年已經過去了，我也該鬆開手、往前走了，
對吧。誰知道，會在台灣一次碰上這麼多烏龜呢？」

"But many years have passed," Marney said,
"it's about time for me to let go, right?
Who knew I would bump into all these turtles in Taiwan?"

聽完了故事，翻譯們恍然大悟。

啊原來，不收烏龜不是因為不喜甜，而是因為捨不得啊。

Ahh, now all the translators understood, so it's not because of sweetness;
it's because no one wants to say bye after all.

「嗯……」第二個翻譯舉手，小小聲地說：
「我家的寵物店昨晚，就是昨晚，
剛剛好進了十隻蘇卡達象龜耶。」
"Well," The second translator said,
"I was at my cousin's pet shop last night,
and they've got 10 Sukada turtles."

「喔……」第三個翻譯笑了，搖了搖頭說：
「我家姪女昨晚找我，就是昨晚，
要我捏給她十隻黏土龜呢。」
"Well," The third translator said,
"My niece came over last night and insisted on
making ten clay turtles."

「瑪妮，你會想留下這個嗎？」第一個翻譯說。
瑪妮拿起小金龜，放在掌心，珍重地看了好一陣子，
然後把他塞回翻譯的手心，像塞回一顆種子。
"Marney, would you maybe want to keep this money turtle?" the first translator asked.
Marney picked up the turtle, weighed it for some quiet moments,
then she put it back into the translator's palm.

「請你好好照顧他，我相信杜克，
我的杜克啊，會給你帶來最好的運氣。」
"You take good care of him," Marney said.
"I believe Duke, my Duke will bring you the best of luck."

那個翻譯擦了擦小金龜，像擦亮古老的神燈。
然後她點點頭，覺得知道了該怎麼做。
The first translator looked at the money turtle,
then nodded, feeling like she knew what to do.

「瑪妮，杜克為什麼喜歡烏龜？」
"Marney, why did Duke like turtles?"

「因為他們不迷路，總可以找回家的方向。」

"Because they are never lost and can always find their way home."

後 記

這個故事發生在 2023 年 5 月，
感謝富邦文教基金會邀請我當隨行口譯，
若非如此，也不會有緣分可以記下這個故事。

然而，想好好畫下小金龜，就得找到他的情緒，
和插畫家一起發呆了許多個下午後，我們終於找到了。

是捨不得吧，亮晶晶的捨不得。
化身為各種烏龜的杜克知道，
當然知道他和瑪妮之間的故事結束了，
但他捨不得啊，想再回頭看一眼，
一眼也好、兩眼也罷，那不然三眼好了你說怎麼樣？
結果最後總共看了三十六頁，多出超多眼的啦。

是飽滿而明亮的，亮晶晶的捨不得，
也是賴皮而感傷的，基本上不顧一切，
你一說好我就出現。

是在恰到好處的陽光下，曬了一下午的好感覺。
是深厚的平靜，是可以像個國王，
慢到不行地點點頭，然後說：
好，那麼就往下一個故事，
走吧。

40

This story took place in May 2023.
Thanks to the Fubon Cultural & Educational Foundation for inviting me to interpret at that time.
Otherwise, I wouldn't have had the serendipity to write this story down.

However, to draw Money Turtle properly, we must understand his emotions and what makes him tick.
After many afternoons staring at blank pages, the illustrator and I finally found it.

It is a sweet sorrow, golden and bright— a reluctance to let go.
Duke, in his various turtle guises, knew, of course, that his story with Marney was over, but he was unable to simply let go. He wants to have one last look at her. Well, one, two, or how about three?
In the end, he spent 36 pages with her, which is much more than expected.

It's the golden feeling after spending a whole afternoon in the sun or the serenity after having your last wish fulfilled.

It's the ability to nod ever so slowly, gracefully like a king, and say,

"Okay then, onto the next story. Let's go!"

作者 / **張江寧 Johnnie Chang**

政治大學歐語學系、臺師大歐文所畢業，
臺師大翻譯研究所口筆譯組躲避論文中。
曾任英語嚮導、全英語教師、報社編譯、影展口筆譯。
第一部小說《床邊昆蟲學》入選 2022 年法蘭克福書展臺灣館、
2024 年義大利波隆那兒童書展臺灣館。

繪者 / **姜硯庭 John**

以繪圖為主的創作者，作品插畫系列《呱啊嘎嘎》畫的是一群笨鳥。
另外還有刺青工作室「this kind of tattoo」以及《玫瑰花計畫》正在進行中。
人生目標是死亡，但是當 Johnnie 找上門來，很高興自己有活到 32 歲。
《找烏龜》是 Johnnie & John 一起完成的第一本繪本，
希望後面還有大約 30 個在排隊。

釀文學 287　PG2998

作者／張江寧 Johnnie Chang
繪者／姜硯庭 John
責任編輯／尹懷君
圖文排版／張家碩
封面設計／張家碩

出版策劃／釀出版
製作發行／秀威資訊科技股份有限公司
114 台北市內湖區瑞光路76巷65號1樓
電話：+886-2-2796-3638
傳真：+886-2-2796-1377
服務信箱：service@showwe.com.tw
http://www.showwe.com.tw

郵政劃撥／19563868
戶名：秀威資訊科技股份有限公司

出版日期／2024年5月　BOD一版

展售門市／國家書店【松江門市】
104台北市中山區松江路209號1樓
電話：+886-2-2518-0207
傳真：+886-2-2518-0778
網路訂購／秀威網路書店：https://store.showwe.tw
　　　　　國家網路書店：https://www.govbooks.com.tw
法律顧問／毛國樑　律師
總經銷／聯合發行股份有限公司
地址：231新北市新店區寶橋路235巷6弄6號4F
電話：+886-2-2917-8022　　傳真：+886-2-2915-6275

定價／450元

讀者回函卡